River

written and illustrated by DEBBY ATWELL

HOUGHTON MIFFLIN COMPANY BOSTON 1999

Walter Lorraine Books

Walter Lorraine (wl) Books

Copyright © 1999 by Debby Atwell

Library of Congress Cataloging-in-Publication Data

Atwell, Debby.
  River / by Debby Atwell
      p.   cm.
    Summary: A river gradually becomes depleted as more and more
people use its resources to build cities, transport goods, and
handle sewage.
    ISBN 0-395-93546-6
    [1. Water pollution — Fiction.   2. Pollution—Fiction.   3. Rivers —
Fiction.]   I. Title.
PZ7.A8935Ri   1999
[E]—dc21   99-10327
                                                                        CIP

Printed in the United States of America
HOR 10 9 8 7 6 5 4 3 2 1

For LISA ANDRESEN

In the beginning there was the river. Trees grew. Fish grew big. And one by one, the animals came to drink the water.

One morning a person appeared. He paddled down the river in a canoe. He knew the river was good. He returned with his family.

After a while more people came. They made friends with the first people. They speared fish together. They traded goods. They shared the river.

Then many new people arrived. They wanted to live on the river too. They fought with the first people. The first people had to leave to find peace.

The new people cleared the land. They used the timber to build houses. They cut down the trees so fast that sometimes there were too many for the river to hold.

More and more people came. Many houses were built. Towns began to grow. The people used the river for fishing, cooking, washing, and traveling.

New inventions changed life for the people. Steamboats took the place of sailing ships. Automobiles took the place of horses. Trains ran beside the waters.

The towns grew bigger, faster and faster. More and more warehouses and factories were built. Businesses boomed.

The animals no longer came to drink. The fish disappeared. There were too many needs.

But the people remembered how it had been. They changed the warehouses. They tore down some of the factories. They planted trees. They wanted to share.

23

One day a person appeared. She paddled up the river in a canoe. She saw that the river was good. She returned with her family.

Again, fish grew big. People used the waters. There was enough for all.

Life had returned to the river. The people had learned to share.

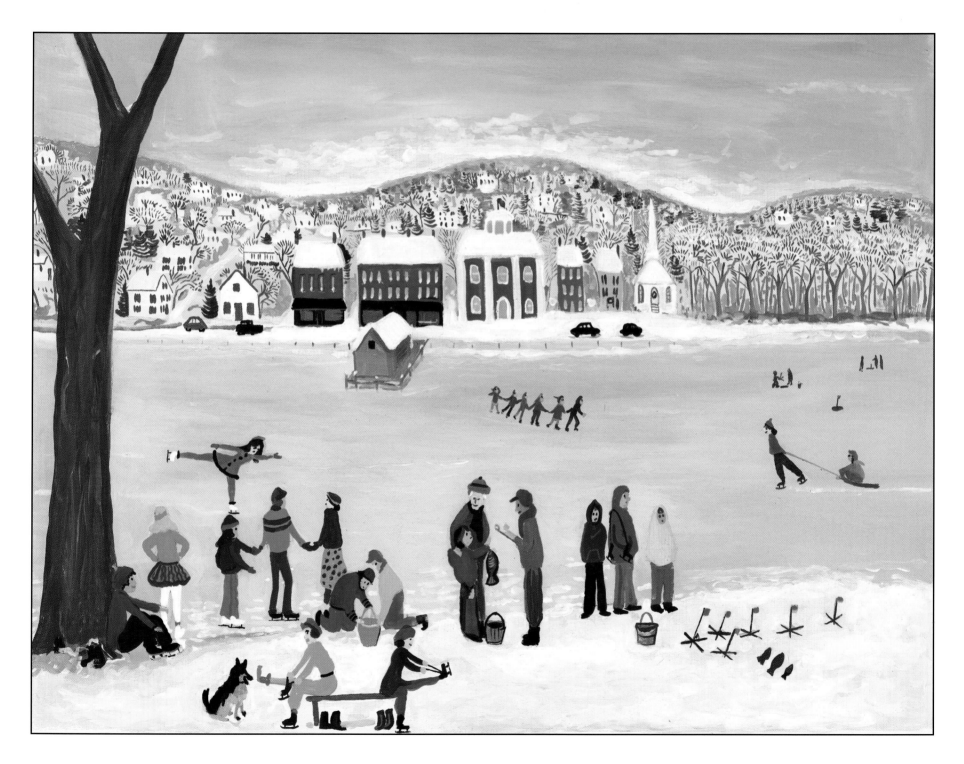